Contents

A Note About These Stories

The stories in this book take place in many different places. *No Comebacks* takes place in London and in Alicante, on the coast of Spain. *There Are Some Days . . .* and *Sharp Practice* are set in Southern Ireland.

The island of Ireland is to the west of Britain and is divided into two. The Republic of Ireland is in the south and is often called Eire. Eire was once part of the United Kingdom. It is now independent. The capital of Eire is Dublin. Northern Ireland is often called Ulster. Ulster is part of the United Kingdom and the capital city is called Belfast. There has been fighting for many years in Northern Ireland; some people do not want Northern Ireland to be part of the United Kingdom.

Ferry-boats cross the sea between Ireland, Britain and Europe every day. As well as passengers, the ferries carry many lorries taking goods to and from Ireland.

A Careful Man is about a millionaire – Timothy Hanson. He owns an apartment in the West End of London and a large office building in the City. The City of London is the centre of business and banking in London. Timothy Hanson lives most of the time in a large country house in the county of Kent, in the south-east of England. He travels by car to his house in Kent. The journey takes him through the East End of London. This is a poorer part of London.

MACMILLAN GUIDED READERS

INTERMEDIATE LEVEL

Series Editor: John Milne

The Macmillan Guided Readers provide a choice of enjoyable reading material for learners of English. The series is published at five levels – Starter, Beginner, Elementary, Intermediate and Upper. At **Intermediate Level**, the control of content and language has the following main features:

Information Control
Information which is vital to the understanding of the story is presented in an easily assimilated manner and is repeated when necessary. Difficult allusion and metaphor are avoided and cultural backgrounds are made explicit.

Structure Control
Most of the structures used in the Readers will be familiar to students who have completed an elementary course of English. Other grammatical features may occur, but their use is made clear through context and reinforcement. This ensures that the reading, as well as being enjoyable, provides a continual learning situation for the students. Sentences are limited in most cases to a maximum of three clauses and within sentences there is a balanced use of simple adverbial and adjectival phrases. Great care is taken with pronoun reference.

Vocabulary Control
There is a basic vocabulary of approximately 1,600 words. Help is given to the students in the form of illustrations, which are closely related to the text.

Glossary
Some difficult words and phrases in this book are important for understanding the story. Some of these words are explained in the story, some are shown in the pictures, and others are marked with a number like this...[3] Words with a number are explained in the Glossary on page 55.

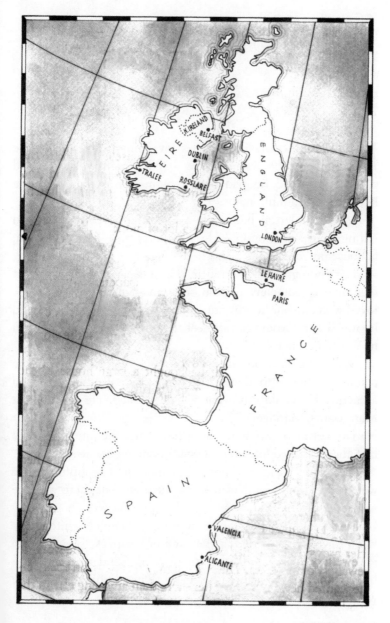

NO COMEBACKS

Mark Sanderson liked to enjoy himself. He liked the company of women. He liked expensive food and champagne. And he had plenty of money to buy what he liked. He was a millionaire.

Mark Sanderson had made a lot of money by buying and selling houses in London. He was thirty-nine years old, rich, famous and bored[1]!

His photograph was often in the newspapers. He was often seen in the company of film stars and famous actresses. He loved women. But he was not in love with one woman. In fact, he was sure he would never meet the one woman – the woman he wanted to marry.

When he became rich, he bought a large house in the country, a house in France, a sports car, a Rolls Royce and a yacht[2]. He could buy whatever he wanted. He said, 'What Mark wants, Mark gets!'

He met many women, but he never met the one woman he had always looked for. Then suddenly, one night, he saw her.

He was at a party. Many rich, famous and beautiful people were there. Mark Sanderson knew them all. But there was one woman there he had never seen before. She was about thirty years old, tall and attractive, wearing a simple[3] white dress. Her brown hair was tied at the back of her neck. She wore no jewellery or make-up. The moment Mark Sanderson saw her– he wanted her. He wanted her more than anything else in the world!

He went up to her and asked, 'Are you enjoying the party?'

The woman smiled at him and replied, 'I don't like it. I was invited here by a school friend, but I don't know anybody.'

Mark Sanderson smiled and looked into her dark eyes. He knew that she was the woman he had waited for. She was the one woman he had thought he would never meet. He also noticed the wedding-ring on her finger.

'Why have I never seen you before?' he asked.

She told him that she lived in Spain. She was in England for only a week. Her husband wrote books. She was an English teacher. Her name was Angela Summers.

At the end of the party, Mark Sanderson invited her to have dinner with him the next evening.

She thought for a moment, then said, 'Yes, I think I'd like that.'

The next evening, he called for[4] her and she came down to the car wearing a long, old-fashioned[5] dress. They drove to a restaurant. During dinner she talked intelligently and listened carefully to what Mark said.

He talked more and more about himself. He liked her very much and wanted to tell her things that he did not often speak about.

They were still talking quietly when the restaurant closed. He asked her to come back with him to his flat. She refused, politely but firmly.

Mark Sanderson was in love. He thought about nothing and about no one except Angela Summers. He sent her presents. He phoned her. He wanted to see her again and again before she went back to Spain. He wanted to show her his house in the country. He wanted to show her his yacht and his cars. He wanted to keep her. 'What Mark wants, Mark gets!'

He wanted to tell her things that he did not often speak about.

On their last evening, he told Angela that he wanted her to stay with him. 'Divorce[6] your husband and marry me,' he said.

She looked at him and saw he was serious. She shook her head and replied, 'I couldn't divorce my husband.'

'I love you,' he said. 'I'll do anything for you.'

'It's my fault,' she said. 'I should have stopped seeing you before now. But you must understand – I could never leave my husband. He needs me.'

'But don't you love me at all?' he asked.

'I don't know,' she said slowly.

'I want you!' Mark said fiercely[7].

'Yes,' she replied. 'But you don't need me. You don't need me the way my husband needs me.'

'So, you'll stay together – you and your husband?' Mark said angrily.

'Yes, for the rest of our lives,' she said quietly. She stood up, kissed him quickly and left.

Mark Sanderson was alone again and still in love. His love was now an obsession[8]. 'What Mark wants, Mark gets,' he said. 'Always.'

———

Mark Sanderson had decided he wanted Angela Summers and he was going to have her. Angela Summers was different from other women. Other women wanted Mark Sanderson's money. But Angela Summers was not interested in money. So, Mark decided to use his money to get her in a different way.

He told his business managers that he was going to have a holiday. He told them he would telephone every day, but he would stay at home. Then he rented[9] a small flat in the middle of London. He paid two months' rent in advance and said his name was 'Michael Johnson' .

From this small flat, he planned how to get Angela Summers. He had a new name – Michael Johnson. Now he needed a new face. His own face was famous. He needed to change it. So, he went to a small hairdresser's and he had his hair cut short and dyed blond[10].

Next, he wanted to know all about Angela Summers and her husband. He paid a detective to find out where they lived in Spain. At the same time, he found the name of a mercenary soldier[11] who had worked for many years in Africa and the Middle East. He found out that the soldier was somewhere in London.

The detective sent information about Angela Summers and her husband. He also sent photographs. Mr and Mrs Summers lived in a villa on the Costa Blanca. Their villa was near the town of Ondara, half-way between Alicante and Valencia. In the mornings, Angela Summers taught English. Every afternoon, between three and four o'clock, she went to the beach. Her husband stayed in the villa. He was writing a book on the birds of southern Spain.

Mark Sanderson owned many companies. Among them was a publishing company which had printed a book on mercenaries in Africa. Mark went to see the author of this book. He took with him the name of the mercenary he wanted to find in London.

The author lived in a cheap flat and was often drunk. Mark Sanderson introduced himself, 'My name's Michael Johnson. I work for your publisher. I enjoyed your book very much.'

'It didn't sell very well,' said the author.

'No . . .' Sanderson agreed, 'but we're thinking of publishing the story of another man – a man you know. We will pay you £100 if you tell us where to find him.'

The author's face lit up when he heard the word money. 'Who do you want to find?'

'Mr Hughes.'

'That bastard[12]! Has he written a book?' the author shouted.

'Where can I find him?' Sanderson asked, counting out ten, ten pound notes.

The author took the money and wrote a name on a piece of paper. 'He drinks there,' was all he said.

Sanderson left. Written on the piece of paper was the name of a bar in Earls Court[13].

That evening, Sanderson sat in the Earls Court bar for five hours. He had no picture of the man he was looking for. But he had a description – tall, strong, broad shoulders, bright eyes and a scar[14] on his jaw. Sanderson recognized the man as soon as he walked in.

The man stood at the bar and drank a pint of beer slowly. When he left, Sanderson followed him. The man walked to a nearby block of flats. He put a key into the door of number 2. He disappeared inside and a light went on in the flat.

Ten minutes later, Sanderson knocked on the door. The light went out in the flat. The door opened slowly. Sanderson could see nothing inside the dark room.

'Mr Hughes?' Sanderson asked.

'Who wants him?' A voice came from the darkness.

'My name's Johnson, Michael Johnson,' said Sanderson.

'Who sent you?'

Sanderson gave the name of the author. The door opened wider.

'Come in.'

Sanderson stepped into the dark room. Hughes closed the door and turned on the light. There was not much furniture in the flat. Hughes pointed to a kitchen chair. Sanderson sat down.

'I want a job done,' Sanderson said. 'I want to have a man killed.'

Hughes looked hard at Sanderson, then went over to a radio which was playing music softly. He turned the volume to maximum, opened a drawer and took out paper, pencil and a gun.

Sanderson felt sick as the gun pointed towards him. Hughes wrote a word on the paper and pushed it across the table. It said: 'STRIP.'

Slowly, Sanderson stood up and took off his jacket. Hughes took it and searched the pockets, still pointing the gun. Sanderson took off the rest of his clothes. Hughes watched.

'All right, get dressed,' Hughes said. He turned down the volume of the radio and put away the gun.

'Did you think I had a gun?' Sanderson asked.

'No,' Hughes replied, 'I wanted to know if you had a microphone or a tape recorder. I could see you hadn't got a gun.'

'Now, about this job,' Sanderson continued. 'I'm prepared to pay well.'

'Not well enough for me,' said Hughes.

'I don't want you.' Sanderson replied. 'I want a foreign mercenary to do a job in a foreign country. Give me the name of a mercenary.'

Sanderson took out fifty new twenty pound notes and put

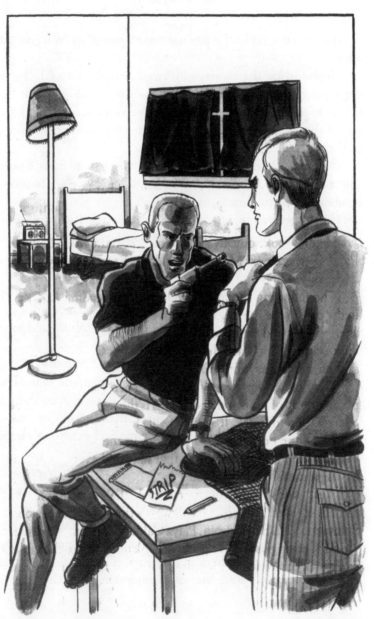

Sanderson felt sick as the gun pointed towards him.

them on the table. 'I'll pay the same again when you give me a name.'

Hughes took the money. 'I'll need a week,' he said. 'Be in the same bar as tonight, one week from today. Be there at ten in the evening. I'll phone you and give you a name. Send the rest of the money, poste restante Hargreaves, to the Post Office in Earls Court.'

One week later, Sanderson was in the bar in Earls Court. The phone rang at 10 o'clock. It was a call for 'Mr Johnson'. Hughes was on the line.

Hughes spoke quickly. 'There's a café in the Rue Miollin in Paris. Be there next Monday at midday. Read *Le Figaro*. Take five thousand pounds cash.'

The following Monday, Sanderson was reading *Le Figaro* in the café in the Rue Miollin. At five past twelve, a man got up from the bar and sat opposite him at his table. The man was a dark skinned Corsican. He said his name was Calvi. Sanderson said his name was Johnson.

They talked for twenty minutes. Then Sanderson put a photo on top of his newspaper. 'This is the man,' he said. 'The address is on the back. It's a quiet villa by the sea. Also the job must be done between three and four in the afternoon, on a weekday. He is always alone at that time and everyone else is having a siesta[15]. Understood?'

'Yes,' said the Corsican. He took the photograph and turned it over. On the back was written: Major Archie Summers, Villa San Crispin, Playa Caldera, Ondara, Alicante.

Sanderson pushed five packs of bank notes across the table. Each pack contained five hundred pounds in fifty pound notes. Calvi quickly wrapped them in *Le Figaro*. 'I'll pay you the same again when you've done the job,' Sanderson said. He wrote a number on a piece of paper. 'Here is a phone number in Paris. Call me as soon as you've done the job. How long?'

'Give me two weeks,' said Calvi.

'Very well,' said Sanderson. 'And, of course, there must be no comebacks – nothing that comes back to me.'

'Of course,' said Calvi, 'there will be no comebacks.'

Calvi looked behind him to make sure he was not followed when he left the café. Then he thought about the job. Should he buy a gun when he got to Spain? Or should he take one with him? He made a decision and went to Iberia airlines and the Spanish tourist office. On his way home, he bought a book and several things from a stationer's shop[16].

That evening, he rang the Hotel Metropol in Valencia and reserved[17] two single rooms for one night. He used the name 'Calvi' and another name on a false passport[18]. He also said he would send a letter to the hotel confirming his reservation.

The letter of confirmation, which he wrote with his left hand, had in it another note, '. . . I have also ordered a book on the history of Spain. Please keep it for me until my arrival. M. Calvi.'

The book, which Calvi had bought that afternoon, was very thick and heavy. It was full of colour photographs.

He opened the book on the kitchen table and started cutting with a sharp knife and a ruler. He cut away the central part of each page, leaving a margin of three centimetres on each side. After an hour, the inside of the book was like a box measuring $20 \times 15 \times 7$ centimetres. Into the box, he carefully put a Browning automatic pistol and a silencer.

He closed the book and put it into a clear plastic envelope. Next, he put this inside a large, brown, padded envelope.

After an hour, the inside of the book was like a box.

He wrote an address on the front:

> M. Calvi,
> c/o Hotel Metropol,
> Valencia,
> Spain.

Ten days later, he flew to Valencia. He used his false passport at the Hotel Metropol.

'Unfortunately, Señor Calvi cannot join me,' he said to the reception clerk, 'but I shall pay for his room and will collect his book.'

'Certainly, señor,' said the reception clerk. He handed over the package addressed to Calvi.

In his room, Calvi looked carefully at the gun. Everything was ready.

The next morning, Calvi checked out of the hotel. He went to the airport and reconfirmed his flight to Paris that evening. Then he went to the car park and waited.

He was looking for businessmen arriving to take the flight to Madrid. Several men arrived, dressed in suits. They parked their cars and walked into the airport carrying briefcases. Calvi followed one of the drivers into the airport.

The man checked in at the departures desk for the flight to Madrid. Calvi returned to the car park. He was an expert car thief. He was soon inside the businessman's car and driving along the road towards Alicante.

Calvi was driving towards the town of Ondara. It took him two hours to reach the town and he arrived at midday. He asked for directions to the Playa Caldera and was told to drive three kilometres out of town. He drove to the beach and found the Villa San Crispin.

The beach was empty. He saw there was a back entrance to the villa which was hidden by orange trees. Through the orange trees he could see a man watering the garden. This was the man he had come to kill. But Calvi was early.

Calvi drove back to Ondara for lunch. The weather was very hot. He was thankful when a dark cloud covered the sun.

He was back on the beach again soon after three o'clock. The job was easier than he thought. The weather helped. Dark clouds covered the sky and there was the noise of thunder. Rain started to fall heavily as he walked through the orange trees to the back of the villa. No one would hear a thing.

The sound of a typewriter came from an open window. Calvi saw the man in the photograph and pulled out his gun. The man looked up when Calvi was only a metre away. Calvi shot him twice in the chest and once in the head. The job was done. He checked the body to make sure the man was dead. Calvi heard a noise and looked at the sitting-room door.

———

In the café in the Rue Miollin in Paris, Sanderson paid another two thousand five hundred pounds to Calvi. 'No problems?' he asked the Corsican gunman. 'No one saw you?'

'No,' said Calvi, 'no witnesses. Someone did come in when I was checking the body.'

'Who?' asked Sanderson, his eyes opening wide in horror.

'A woman.

'Yeah. Nice looking,' said Calvi, who saw the look of horror on the other man's face. 'Don't worry. There'll be no comebacks. I shot her too.'

THERE ARE SOME DAYS . . .

The ferry from Le Havre in France sailed into Rosslare harbour in the Republic of Ireland. The ship was full of passengers with cars and also lorries loaded with goods.

Liam Clarke was a lorry driver. He had loaded his lorry in Belgium and now he was going home to Dublin. He hoped to be home before evening.

The ship docked[19] and the cargo doors opened. Liam climbed into his green and white Volvo lorry, started the engine and drove onto the dockside. There was so much noise that he did not hear a sharp cracking sound from underneath the lorry.

He drove along the dockside to the customs shed[20] and stopped the lorry's engine. A customs officer came to inspect his import documents. The officer pointed under the lorry and asked, 'What's that?'

Liam climbed out of his lorry and looked underneath. He saw thick black oil running out of the engine. There was already half a litre on the ground and more oil ran out as he watched.

'Your lorry won't move far,' said the customs officer. 'You'll have to leave it here and get a mechanic[21] to repair it.'

The customs officer went to inspect other lorries. Liam went to the nearest phone and called his boss in Dublin. He told him that his lorry had broken down.

'You'll have to stay in Rosslare tonight,' said his boss. 'I'll send a mechanic with spare parts tomorrow morning.'

So Liam Clarke left his green and white Volvo in the customs shed and found a bed and breakfast lodging-house for the night. Next morning, he went back to the harbour and waited for the mechanic. The mechanic did not arrive until midday.

'How long will it take to repair the lorry?' Liam asked.

'A couple of hours,' replied the mechanic. 'You'll be home before evening.'

The mechanic started work. He was finishing the repair when the afternoon ferry from France sailed into Rosslare harbour.

———

Up on a hill above Rosslare, two men were watching the ferry sail into the harbour.

'Here she comes, right on time,' Murphy said to Brendan. 'Look for a green and white lorry coming off the ship.'

Brendan looked through a pair of binoculars[22]. The first lorry to come off the ship was brown with a French licence number. The second lorry was bright green and white with the word TARA on the trailer.

'That's it! That's the one!' said Brendan. 'Shall we go now?'

'There's no hurry,' said Murphy. 'We'll wait to see it come out of the customs shed first. We want the customs to check that there's nine thousand bottles of best French brandy in that lorry, don't we?'

'It's a lot of brandy,' said Brendan.

'It's a lot of money,' said Murphy. 'We're going to sell it, not drink it!'

'Here she comes, right on time,' Murphy said to Brendan.

The green and white lorry drove into the customs shed and stopped next to Liam's lorry. Both lorries were the same colour. Both lorries had the company name TARA on their trailers.

The driver of the second lorry put his head out of the window and spoke to Liam Clarke. 'What the hell[23] happened to you, Liam?'

'I had a breakdown,' said Liam, 'but it's fixed now.' He turned to a customs officer. 'Can I go?'

'Yes, go ahead,' said the customs officer.

Liam drove the heavy lorry out of the harbour and went north along the Dublin road. He did not notice the black Ford Granada which drove behind him. Murphy and Brendan were in the Granada.

'He came through customs quickly,' said Brendan.

'Yes, he did,' said Murphy. 'Stop at the next phone box.'

They stopped for Murphy to make a phone call. 'The lorry is coming,' Murphy said on the phone to the two other members of his gang. 'Be ready.'

The black Granada followed Liam's lorry for a few kilometres then turned into a narrow country road. Murphy and Brendan quickly put on policemen's uniforms. They stuck two strips of black plastic to the sides of their car. Each strip had the word GARDA[24] in white letters. The black Ford Granada now looked exactly like a police car.

Murphy and Brendan raced after the green and white lorry. They drove behind it for several kilometres, waiting for the right moment. Soon they saw a road sign – PARKING 1 KM.

'Now!' said Murphy. The car drove faster and overtook[25] the lorry.

Liam Clarke saw a police car overtake his lorry and a policeman waving at him to stop. He also saw a parking sign by the roadside. He slowed down, drove into the parking place and stopped.

'Look at your back wheel,' said one of the policemen, as he got out of the GARDA car.

Liam got out of his lorry and followed the policemen round to the back. Suddenly, two men jumped out of the bushes beside the road and grabbed him.

They stuck sticky tape over Liam's mouth and eyes and round his hands. Then they pushed him into the back of the police car.

Murphy and Brendan pulled the GARDA signs off the black car. They took off their police helmets and jackets. They threw these into the back of the car on top of Liam.

Murphy turned to the two other members of his gang. 'Drive the lorry to the farm,' he said. 'We'll see you there.'

Murphy and Brendan drove away in the black car. The two men climbed into the lorry and followed them.

The farm was away from the main road. It was along a muddy track and had a large barn[26] beside it. Brendan pulled Liam Clarke out of the car and pushed him into the farmhouse kitchen. The lorry drove into the barn and the men closed the barn doors. Then the four men sat in the farmhouse and waited.

It was dark soon after six o'clock. At eight o'clock, Murphy went to the end of the muddy track and shone a torch. Four vans, with Northern Ireland licence numbers, drove up the track. The vans stopped in front of the barn. A big man got out of one of the vans carrying a briefcase.

'Have you got the brandy?' asked the big man from the North.

'Yes,' said Murphy. 'It's in the barn. I've not touched it.'

'Good,' said the man from the North. He turned to his men. 'Load it up,' he said. Then he spoke to Murphy. 'Let's go inside.'

Inside the farmhouse, the Northerner opened his briefcase. It was full of ten pound notes.

'Nine thousand bottles of brandy at four pounds a bottle, that's thirty-six thousand pounds,' said Murphy.

'Thirty-five,' said the Northerner.

Murphy didn't argue.

One of the other Northerners came to the door and spoke to his boss.

'You'd better come and look.'

The big man closed the briefcase and carried it outside.

Murphy followed the big man to the barn. Six men were shining torches into the lorry. The lorry was full of plastic sacks.

'Where's the driver?' asked the big man angrily.

Murphy took the Northerner into the kitchen. Liam Clarke, the lorry driver, was sitting in the corner with tape over his eyes and mouth.

'What the hell have you got in your lorry?' shouted the big man, tearing the tape from Liam's mouth.

'Bags of fertilizer[27],' Liam said. 'It's written on the customs documents.'

The big man grabbed the pile of papers from Murphy's hand and looked at the customs documents. 'Did you not look at this, you fool?' he asked Murphy.

Murphy was frightened. 'There was only one TARA lorry that came off the ferry from France,' he said. 'We know there was brandy on that lorry. We had a message from France. Isn't there any brandy under the fertilizer?'

'What the hell have you got in your lorry?' shouted the big
man, tearing the tape from Liam's mouth.

'Brandy?' Liam said, 'Why do you think there's any brandy? I'm carrying a load of fertilizer, that's all.'

The big man turned to Murphy. 'Listen,' he said, 'you have wasted[28] my men's time and my money. If you ever do anything like this again – you're dead! Do you understand me?'

The big man walked out and told his men to get into their vans. Five minutes later, the men from the North had gone.

'What do we do now?' Brendan asked Murphy.

'You take the lorry driver and leave him beside the main road to Dublin,' Murphy said. 'I'll take the lorry and hide it up in the hills. Then we'll meet in Dublin tomorrow.'

The doors of the lorry trailer had been broken. Murphy closed them with a piece of wood. Then he drove the lorry through narrow lanes up into the hills.

It was a dark night and Murphy did not think there would be any traffic on the country lanes. But suddenly, in front of him, he saw a farm tractor pulling a load of straw[29]. Murphy tried to stop the lorry, but it was too late.

The lorry ran into the load of straw and the lorry trailer swung round, hitting a stone wall. The farmer was knocked off his tractor and the front of the lorry was covered in straw.

Murphy pushed the lorry door open and climbed out. The farmer was on the ground, shouting and swearing. But he was not hurt. Murphy went to help him when suddenly he saw the headlights of another car – a car with a blue light on top. It was a police car.

This was amazing. What was a police car doing at night in the middle of the countryside?

Two policemen got out of their car and looked at the tractor and the lorry. 'Show us your papers,' one of them said

*The lorry ran into the load of straw and the lorry trailer
swung round, hitting a stone wall.*

to Murphy. Murphy gave them Liam Clarke's customs papers and waited, silently.

The farmer went on shouting and swearing until a police man said, 'There are no lights on this tractor. It's against the law to drive a tractor without lights.'

The farmer shut up[30] quickly. The police were now more interested in the farmer than in Murphy.

'Clear this straw off the road,' said the policeman. 'You can't drive this tractor, but you can let this lorry go through.'

Murphy was happy.

'What's your cargo?' one of the policemen asked.

'Fertilizer,' Murphy replied.

The policeman laughed. 'Right. Some sacks have fallen out of the back door. Put them in the lorry and you can go.'

'Thanks,' said Murphy and walked to the back of the lorry where the trailer doors were open. Several of the large sacks had burst open. The policemen shone their torches on the sacks in the roadway.

'What's this?' one of them asked in surprise.

In the torchlight, Murphy saw that there was not only fertilizer in the burst sacks. He saw a bazooka[31] and several machine guns.

Murphy took a deep breath. There are some days when nothing goes right. He had tried to hijack[32] nine thousand bottles of French brandy. Instead, he had hijacked a cargo of machine guns! And he knew that the owners of the guns would not be pleased. Suddenly, he felt safer being with the police.

A CAREFUL MAN

Timothy Hanson sat in his doctor's office at an expensive clinic[33] in London. The doctor had made many tests and taken many X-rays.

'I am sorry to tell you, Mr Hanson,' said the doctor, 'you have terminal cancer. You have only six months to live.'

Timothy Hanson smiled at the doctor. 'Thank you for telling me,' he said. Then he stood up, shook hands with the doctor and left the clinic.

Timothy Hanson's Rolls Royce was waiting outside the clinic. His chauffeur opened the car door and asked, 'To the office, Mr Hanson?'

'No,' Hanson replied. 'Drive me home, please.'

The car drove east and Timothy Hanson looked out of the window at the buildings, shops and offices of central London. He thought about all the buildings and all the money he owned. He was a very rich man, but he was dying.

I must make a will[34], he thought to himself.

As they drove through the East End of London, the buildings became poorer. The car stopped in the Old Kent Road as a line of children crossed the road. Two nuns[35] walked at the front of the line and two more nuns followed at the back.

A small boy stopped in the middle of the road and stared at the Rolls Royce. He wore a school cap with the initials 'St. B.' on it. His hair was untidy and so were his clothes. He stared at the silver-haired man in the Rolls Royce. Then he put the thumb of his right hand to his nose and waggled[36] his fingers at Timothy Hanson.

Timothy Hanson stared back at the boy. Then he put the thumb of his right hand to his nose and waggled his fingers in reply. The chauffeur was amazed. The boy in the middle of the road was surprised. A huge smile lit up his face.

A second later, a young nun pulled the boy across the road. The Rolls Royce drove on towards Timothy Hanson's country house.

Timothy Hanson was thinking about making a will. Who would he leave his money to? Whoever got his money would have to pay a lot of tax to the government. His wife was dead and he had no children. There was only one member of his family left – his sister. She was an unpleasant woman who had an unpleasant husband and an unpleasant son.

Timothy Hanson had six months to make all the final arrangements.

———

Six months later, Mr and Mrs Armitage sat in a lawyer's office with their son, Tarquin. All of them were wearing black clothes. Mr Timothy Hanson was dead.

The lawyer came in and sat down. He held a large envelope in his hand. 'Mr Hanson wanted you to hear his will immediately after his death,' the lawyer said.

'What – just the three of us?' asked Mr Armitage.

'Yes,' replied the lawyer. 'You are Mr Hanson's only relatives, I believe.'

'Then all his money is coming to us,' said Tarquin greedily.

'Shut up, dear,' said Mrs Armitage.

'Let's hear the will immediately,' Tarquin said.

The lawyer opened the large envelope carefully. Inside was

He put the thumb of his right hand to his nose and waggled his fingers.

another envelope and a sheet of paper. The lawyer began to read the sheet of paper, 'This is the last will and testament of me, Timothy John Hanson, of . . .'

'We know all that,' said Mr Armitage.

'Get on with it,' said Mrs Armitage.

'Tell us how much money we've got,' said Tarquin Armitage.

The lawyer continued, 'There is an envelope enclosed, in which there is five thousand pounds. This will pay the costs of my burial[37] and of my lawyer. The rest of my estate[38] I leave to my sister, her husband and their son Tarquin, after . . .'

'How much?' said Mr Armitage quickly.

'I don't know,' the lawyer replied.

'You must know,' said Mrs Armitage.

'Yeah, you must know,' said Tarquin Armitage.

'Well . . .' said the lawyer, 'the estate is probably worth about three million pounds.'

'Good heavens,' said Mr Armitage. 'How much tax will we have to pay to the government?'

'About sixty-five per cent,' replied the lawyer.

'That leaves us a million!' shouted Tarquin Armitage.

'About a million,' said the lawyer. 'Now, may I read the last paragraph of the will?'

'Go on,' said Mrs Armitage. 'What does it say?'

'. . . after my death,' the lawyer continued. 'I wish to be buried at sea. I have prepared a special lead[39] coffin for my burial. My relatives shall arrange my burial at sea. I want to be buried thirty kilometres south of the Devon coast in deep water.'

'He wants to be buried in a special lead coffin, at sea?' asked Mrs Armitage. 'Is a burial at sea allowed by the law?'

'Yes, it is perfectly legal,' said the lawyer. 'Also, there is one more thing.'

'What?' asked Mrs Armitage.

'My relatives shall receive my estate on the day after my burial,' the lawyer continued to read. 'Also, they must agree to follow my instructions exactly. If they do not agree, I will leave all my estate to the government.'

'Is that all?' asked Mrs Armitage.

'Yes,' replied the lawyer. 'Do you agree to follow your brother's instructions?'

'Well, I don't know,' said Mrs Armitage. 'How much will it cost?'

'This money will pay for it,' said the lawyer, holding up the envelope in which there was five thousand pounds. If you do not agree, you will not receive your brother's estate. All his money will go to the government.'

'I agree,' said Mrs Armitage quickly.

A week later, the Armitages were on a small fishing boat in the English Channel. The sea was rough, and the Armitages felt sick. The lawyer was with them together with a priest. Timothy Hanson's body was in a very heavy lead coffin. The coffin had been brought on board the fishing boat and it now stood on the deck.

'We're coming to deep water now,' said the captain of the fishing boat. The coffin was moved to the edge of the deck. The Armitages stood round and the priest began to pray.

The lead coffin was very heavy. All of them had to push together to move it over the edge of the deck.

All of them had to push together to move the coffin over the edge of the deck.

Finally the coffin moved and fell into the sea with a great splash. The boat turned and sailed back to the port.

'We want to know as quickly as possible how much money we've got,' said Mrs Armitage.

'I shall let you know as soon as possible,' said the lawyer.

Two weeks later, Mrs Armitage was sitting in the lawyer's office again. Her husband and son sat beside her.

'There is a problem,' the lawyer told them.

'Haven't you found out how much my brother's estate is worth?' asked Mrs Armitage angrily.

'No,' replied the lawyer. 'I know how much your brother's estate was worth.'

'WAS?' shouted Mrs Armitage. 'What do you mean?'

'Well, Mr Hanson sold everything before he died,' said the lawyer.

'And what did he do with the money?' asked Tarquin Armitage.

'He put it in the bank,' replied the lawyer.

'And where is it now?' asked Mr Armitage.

'That,' said the lawyer, 'is the problem. He took it out of the bank.'

'How much?' asked Mrs Armitage.

'Three million pounds,' said the lawyer.

'And where is it now?' asked Tarquin.

'I don't know,' the lawyer replied.

There was silence in the room. The Armitages were horrified.

'He's hidden it,' said Mrs Armitage. 'He's hidden three million pounds of my money!'

'Of course, the government will try to find the money,' said the lawyer. 'Remember you owe the government sixty-five per cent in tax.'

'How can we find it?' asked Mr Armitage. 'Can we ask a detective to find it?'

'That's possible,' said the lawyer. 'You will have to pay the detective.'

'Er . . . yes,' said Mr Armitage. 'All right. We'll pay him.'

'Then I'll arrange it,' the lawyer said.

———

A month later, they all met in the lawyer's office again. There was a detective with the lawyer.

'This is Mr Miller,' said the lawyer. 'He has found out part of the story. He knows where your brother's money went to after it left the bank. But he does not know where it went to in the end.'

'Let's hear the story,' said Mrs Armitage.

Mr Miller stood up to speak. 'I thought at first that your brother had bought something with his money.'

'What? Gold? Diamonds?' asked Mrs Armitage.

'Yes,' Mr Miller replied. 'That's what I thought. But I was wrong. He didn't buy gold or diamonds. Your brother bought bars of platinum[40].'

'Platinum?' asked Mrs Armitage. 'Why platinum?'

'Because, it is against the law to keep a lot of gold,' said Mr Miller. 'But there is no law against keeping large amounts of platinum. And platinum is worth as much as gold.'

'Where did he keep all this platinum?' asked Mr Armitage.

'At his country house in Kent,' said Miller. 'He had a workshop behind the house and a small furnace[41].'

'Do you think he melted the platinum in the furnace?' asked the lawyer.

'I'm sure he did,' replied Miller. 'Platinum is an extremely heavy metal, like gold or lead. It would be very difficult to move such a large amount of platinum. But I believe Mr Hanson melted the metal and made it into the shape of a box or crate.'

'Or a coffin!' screamed Mrs Armitage. She remembered her brother's unusual burial and the very heavy 'lead' coffin. 'The bastard has taken all his money with him to the bottom of the sea!'

———

A scrap metal dealer[42] walked happily towards the bank. He had just sold a large number of platinum bars. He had bought the platinum bars from a silver-haired man about three months earlier. The silver-haired man had not wanted to pay tax to the government. The scrap metal dealer had offered a low price in cash. He had asked no questions and did not know the silver-haired man's name. Both men had been happy with the deal. The scrap metal dealer had made several thousand pounds profit by reselling the metal.

In different parts of Britain there were four other metal dealers who were also happy. They had bought platinum from a silver-haired man, about three months ago, for cash. They had all made a big profit by reselling the metal. None of them had asked any questions. It would not now be possible for anyone to find the metal again.

———

On the day before Christmas, a lawyer from Guernsey[43] walked into Saint Benedict's Orphanage in the Old Kent Road in the East End of London. He asked to see the Mother Superior. When he went into her office, he gave her an envelope.

'I have been instructed to give you this envelope,' said the lawyer. 'I cannot tell you who gave me the instructions.'

'What is it?' asked the Mother Superior.

'It is a cheque,' said the lawyer. 'It is a cheque from a bank in Guernsey. It is money for the orphanage.'

'Why is it from Guernsey?' asked the Mother Superior.

'In Guernsey, the law is different from the law in England,' said the lawyer. 'There is no tax to pay on this money. Now, would you please sign these papers?'

The lawyer left. The Mother Superior looked at the cheque again. It was a cheque for two and half million pounds. So much money! The Mother Superior could not believe it.

What was she going to do with so much money? She had always wanted to move the orphanage to the countryside, away from the East End of London. She looked at the property pages of the morning newspaper 'For Sale. Country House in Kent. Five hectares of parkland. Previously owned by Mr T. J. Hanson.'

'What is it?' asked the Mother Superior.

SHARP PRACTICE

Fifty years ago, Judge Comyn sat in a first class railway compartment[44] reading the *Irish Times*. The train was about to leave Dublin on its four hour journey to Tralee. Judge Comyn was going to be the judge at the County Court.

A small man came into the compartment and sat opposite the judge. Then, just before the train left the station, a red-faced priest joined them, breathing heavily.

'You almost missed the train, Father,' said the small man.

'Yes, my son,' the priest replied, 'I had to run to catch it.'

At first, the three strangers were silent. The judge read some legal papers which he had put on the table in front of him.

'Excuse me,' said the small man. 'Do you mind if I use the edge of the table?'

'You're welcome, certainly,' said the judge.

'Thank you, sir,' said the small man. He took a pack of cards out of his pocket and started to play patience[45] on the table.

The judge tried to read his legal papers, but he kept looking at the game of patience. The small man was playing badly.

Finally, the judge spoke. 'Put that king on the queen and you can finish the game.'

'Thank you sir,' said the small man, 'but I've never finished a game of patience in my life.'

The priest had put down his book to watch the end of the game.

'You will, you will,' said the judge. 'Put the red nine on the

40

black ten. There you are, you see, you've finished.'

'But only with your help, sir,' said the small man. 'I can tell that you are good at cards.'

'Thank you,' said the judge, feeling pleased with himself.

The small man began to deal hands of poker[46] on the table. He looked at each hand carefully then put the cards down.

Time passed. After a while, the small man grew tired of playing cards by himself. He put the cards down. 'It's a long way to Tralee,' he said.

'I saw you were dealing hands of poker,' said the judge. 'Perhaps we could play a few hands of poker together?'

'Of course,' said the small man. 'My name's O'Connor.'

'And my name's Comyn,' said the judge.

They dealt a few poker hands and looked at them. Of course, they were not playing for money.

'We need some way of counting who has won,' said O'Connor.

'I've got some matches,' said Judge Comyn.

'That's what we need,' said O'Connor. The judge counted out twenty matchsticks each.

It is difficult to play poker with only two players. After a time, O'Connor asked the priest, 'Father, would you like to play with us?'

'Oh, no,' said the red-faced priest with a laugh. 'I don't know how to play.'

'It's not a difficult game,' said O'Connor. 'You get five cards from the dealer at the beginning of each game. At the beginning, you can ask the dealer to change three of your cards, to try to make a better hand. If your hand is good, you bet on it. If your hand is bad, you fold – which means you put the cards down and don't bet any more.'

'Bet?' asked the priest. 'Do you mean play for money?'

'Oh, no, Father,' O'Connor smiled. 'We're only playing for matchsticks.'

'But I don't know what is a good hand and what is a bad one,' said the priest.

'I'll write down the hands,' said O'Connor. He took a pencil and a piece of paper from his pocket. 'Keep this paper on the table, so you'll know what a hand is worth.'

'Very well,' said the priest. 'I'll play for matchsticks.'

For the first two games, the priest had bad hands. So he folded and watched the other two bet. The judge won four matchsticks. Then, on the third game, the priest's face lit up.

'Is this not good?' asked the priest, showing three jacks and two kings.

The judge looked angry and put his cards on the table.

'Yes, Father,' said O'Connor quietly. 'It's a good hand, but you must not show us until we've finished betting.'

'Oh, I'm sorry,' said the priest.

They played for an hour. The judge won nearly all the matchsticks and was pleased with himself.

'It's not very interesting playing with matches,' said O'Connor.

'I've enjoyed the game,' said the judge.

'Perhaps we could make it more interesting,' said O'Connor. 'Why don't we bet for a few shillings?'

'If you like,' said the judge. 'But your luck[47] is bad today.'

'My luck must change,' smiled O'Connor.

'I cannot gamble,' said the priest. 'I cannot play for money. It's a sin[48].'

The judge thought for a moment, then said, 'Mr O'Connor, shall we lend the Father some money? If he

'Is this not good?' asked the priest, showing three jacks and two kings.

loses, we shall not ask him to return the money. If he wins, he can pay it back.'

'An excellent idea,' O'Connor agreed.

'No, no,' said the priest. 'I cannot play for money.'

'But,' said the judge, 'if you win, you can give the money to charity[49].'

The priest thought for a moment or two. 'I'm not sure,' he said. 'Well, I'm going to visit an orphanage and they need some money. Yes, I could play if the money is for charity.'

'Excellent,' said the judge. 'Now, Mr O'Connor, how much shall we play for? How much is one matchstick worth?'

'Ten shillings,' said O'Connor. The judge was surprised. Ten shillings was a lot of money.

They began to play again, but now the matchsticks were worth money. The priest was lucky and won matchsticks from both the judge and O'Connor. He paid back the money they had lent him in the beginning.

Shortly before the train reached Tralee, the judge got a very good hand – four queens. He bet ten pounds, then another ten. O'Connor folded. The priest was still in the game and bet all his money.

'I'm sorry, Father,' said the judge, turning over his cards. 'I have four queens.'

'What a pity,' said the priest. 'I was hoping to give the money to the orphans. Does your hand beat this?'

The priest turned over his hand – four kings.

'I owe you fifty pounds,' said the judge, writing out a cheque. 'The bank will give you fifty pounds in cash for this cheque.'

'And I owe you this,' said O'Connor, handing over twelve one pound notes.

'Bless you,' said the priest. 'The orphanage will be pleased to have so much money.'

The train arrived at Tralee.

Judge Comyn stayed the night at a hotel. He went to the courthouse before nine o'clock the next morning. His first two cases were simple and easy to decide. The third case was about gambling and cheating at cards.

'Call Ronan O'Connor,' shouted the clerk of the court.

Judge Comyn looked up and saw the man he had played cards with on the train. O'Connor looked back at the judge in amazement.

'Are you guilty or not guilty?' asked the judge.

'Not guilty,' said O'Connor.

A lawyer told the court the case against[50] Mr O'Connor. On 13th May, Lurgan Keane, a grocer from Tralee, had travelled on the train from Dublin to Tralee. He had played poker with O'Connor and lost sixty two pounds. At Tralee railway station, Keane had called the police. He said that O'Connor had cheated him and the police arrested O'Connor. They found a special pack of cards in O'Connor's pocket. The cards were cut and marked in a special way so that they could be used for cheating.

O'Connor did not want a lawyer to help him. He stood up and asked Lurgan Keane some questions.

'Did I speak to you first on the train?' he asked.

Lurgan Keane thought for a moment. 'No, I spoke to you, because you were playing patience so badly.'

Judge Comyn put his hand over his eyes.

'So,' O'Connor went on, 'you spoke to me first, and you also suggested playing poker for money.'

'No,' said Lurgan Keane, 'you suggested playing poker.'

'But for matchsticks,' said O'Connor. 'I suggested playing poker for matchsticks. It was you who suggested playing for money.'

Lurgan Keane thought again. 'Yes, perhaps it was,' he said. 'But,' he turned to Judge Comyn, 'isn't it a trick, sir? The cheat gets the other man to suggest playing for money.'

'Money?' O'Connor said loudly. 'How much money did you pay me?'

'Sixty-two pounds,' said Keane angrily.

'No,' said O'Connor, 'how much money did you pay me?'

Lurgan Keane thought carefully. 'I didn't pay you any money. I paid the farmer. It was the farmer who won.'

'And did I win money from the farmer?' asked O'Connor.

'No,' said Lurgan Keane. 'You lost about eight pounds to the farmer.'

'No more questions,' said O'Connor.

The judge spoke to Lurgan Keane. 'Who was the farmer?'

'The other man in the train compartment, sir,' said Lurgan Keane. 'He was a bad poker player, but he had good luck.'

'What was his name?' asked the judge.

'I don't know,' answered Keane. 'He was a farmer from Wexford. He almost missed the train at Dublin. But it wasn't him who cheated me. It was O'Connor. O'Connor had the cards. O'Connor was the cheat!'

The judge thought for a moment, then spoke. 'We have been told that Mr O'Connor won money by cheating at cards. The police took a pack of cards from Mr O'Connor. Mr O'Connor told the police he found the pack of cards on the train. Also, we have heard that Mr O'Connor did not win money from Mr Keane. In fact, both men lost money to an unknown farmer from Wexford. The case against Mr

O'Connor is not proved[51]. I find Mr O'Connor not guilty.'

Everyone in the courtroom stood up as the judge left. It was time for lunch.

Judge Comyn went to his room at the back of the court house and took off his robe. He went out of the courthouse and crossed the road to the town's main hotel.

Lurgan Keane was standing on the pavement staring at an expensive car that was leaving the hotel. Judge Comyn stood beside him and looked into the car.

O'Connor was driving. Beside him sat the priest who had played cards with the judge on the train. The priest waved to the judge.

'Why is he dressed in those clothes?' asked Lurgan Keane.

'Because he's a priest,' answered the judge.

'No he's not,' said Lurgan Keane. 'He's the farmer from Wexford.'

O'Connor was driving. Beside him sat the priest who had
played cards with the judge.

POINTS
FOR
UNDERSTANDING

Points For Understanding

NO COMEBACKS

1 How wealthy was Mark Sanderson?
2 Complete the blanks in the following sentence: Mark Sanderson was thirty-nine years old, . . ., . . . and . . .
3 Sanderson met a woman at a party. Describe this woman.
4 Why had Sanderson never seen this woman before?
5 What did Sanderson say to Angela on their last evening together?
6 Why did Angela say she had to stay with her husband?
7 Complete the following: 'What Mark wants, ...'
8 Sanderson paid a detective to find out about Angela and her husband.
   (a)   Where did Angela and her husband live?
   (b)   What town was the villa near?
   (c)   What did Angela do every afternoon?
   (d)   What did her husband do in the afternoon?
9 Sanderson went to visit an author.
   (a)   What had this author written a book about?
   (b)   Why did Mark offer this author £100?
   (c)   What did the author give Mark?
10 Why did Sanderson go to a bar in Earls Court?
11 What did Sanderson tell Hughes he wanted done?
12 Hughes wrote a word on a piece of paper and gave it to Sanderson.
   (a)   What was the word on the paper?
   (b)   Why did Sanderson feel sick?
   (c)   What had Hughes wanted to find out?
13 What did Sanderson want Hughes to give him?
14 How much did Sanderson offer to pay Hughes:
   (a)   that night?
   (b)   after Sanderson was given what he wanted?

15 A week later, Sanderson got a message by phone.
    (a)   Where was he when he got the message?
    (b)   What city was he to go to?
    (c)   Where was he to go in that city?
    (d)   When was he to be there?
    (e)   What was he to read?
    (f)   How much money was he to take with him?
16 Sanderson gave Calvi a photograph.
    (a)   What was on the back of the photograph?
    (b)   When was the job to be done?
    (c)   Why was the job to be done at that time?
17 What did Sanderson say there must not be?
18 How did Calvi hide a pistol and a silencer?
19 Why did he book two rooms at the Hotel Metropol and then say that Señor Calvi could not join him?
20 Where was the Hotel Metropol?
21 Why did Calvi steal a car from a businessman taking a flight to Madrid?
22 Where did Calvi have lunch?
23 The job was easier than Calvi thought.
    (a)   In what way had the weather helped the job?
    (b)   In what way had the weather made sure 'There'll be no comebacks?'
    (c)   Explain the title of this story.

THERE ARE SOME DAYS . . .

1 Describe the lorry which Liam Clarke was driving.
2 'Your lorry won't move far,' said the customs officer.
    (a)   Where was Liam's lorry?
    (b)   Why would it not move very far?
    (c)   Where did Liam stay for the night?
3 What happened as the mechanic was finishing the repair to Liam's lorry?
4 Describe the lorry Murphy and Brendan were waiting for.
5 How many bottles of brandy were in this lorry?
6 A black Ford Granada followed Liam's lorry.
    (a)   Who was in the Ford Granada?
    (b)   Why were they following Liam's lorry?

7 Describe how Murphy and Brendan stopped Liam's lorry.
8 How was Liam kidnapped?
9 Where was Liam's lorry hidden?
10 What did Murphy do at eight o'clock?
11 How many vans drove up the track? What kind of licence numbers did they have?
12 How much money was the Northerner going to pay Murphy?
13 Explain in detail why the Northerner did not pay Murphy any money at all.
14 What did Murphy tell Brendan to do with Liam?
15 Why was Murphy going too fast?
16 What was the farmer doing which was against the law?
17 The policemen shone their torches on the sacks in the roadway.
   (a)   What had Murphy tried to hijack?
   (b)   What had he hijacked instead?
   (c)   Why did Murphy feel safer with the police?

A CAREFUL MAN

1 What did the doctor tell Timothy Hanson?
2 Why did Timothy Hanson have to make a will?
3 The car stopped in the Old Kent Road.
   (a)   Why did the car have to stop?
   (b)   What were the initials on the schoolboy's cap?
   (c)   What did the schoolboy do to make fun of Timothy Hanson?
   (d)   What did Timothy Hanson do in reply?
4 Who would get a lot of Timothy Hanson's money whoever he left it to?
5 There was only one member of Timothy Hanson's family left.
   (a)   Who was she?
   (b)   What kind of person was she? What kind of people were her husband and her son?
6 Why did Tarquin Armitage think all Timothy Hanson's money was coming to them?
7 'There is an envelope enclosed . . .' said the lawyer.
   (a)   How much money was in the envelope?
   (b)   What was this money to be used for?
8 How much money did the lawyer say the estate was probably worth? How much tax would have to be paid?

9 Describe in detail where and how Timothy Hanson was to be buried.

10 When were the Armitages to get Timothy Hanson's money?

11 What was to happen to Timothy Hanson's money if the Armitages did not agree to bury him exactly as he requested?

12 The sea was rough and the Armitages felt sick.
   (a) Where were the Armitages?
   (b) Why was the coffin extremely heavy?

13 'There is a problem,' the lawyer told them.
   (a) What is the problem?
   (b) What did Mrs Armitage think Timothy Hanson had done with the money?

14 What did the detective tell the Armitages Timothy Hanson had done with the money?

15 What did Mrs Armitage think Timothy Hanson had done with his money?

16 What had a scrap metal dealer bought from a silver-haired man?

17 Why had the silver-haired man accepted a low price in cash?

18 Why would it not be possible for anyone to find the metal again?

19 What is the connection between Saint Benedict's Orphanage and the small boy who put his thumb to his nose?

20 Why was there no tax to pay on the gift to the Orphanage?

21 How much was the gift for?

22 What had the Mother Superior always wanted to do?

23 Do you think Timothy Hanson would be pleased if the Mother Superior bought the house she saw advertised in the morning newspaper?

SHARP PRACTICE

1 How long was the journey from Dublin to Tralee?

2 Who got in the compartment with the judge?

3 What game of cards did the small man start to play to pass the time?

4 Why did the judge speak to the small man?

5 Why did the judge feel pleased with himself?

6 What game of cards did the small man start to play next?

7 Who suggested that they played poker?

8 Why did they use matchsticks?

9 Who suggested that the priest played cards with them?

10 What two reasons did the priest give for not wanting to play?

11 How did O'Connor persuade the priest to play?

12 What did O'Connor tell the priest he must not do?

13 The priest was persuaded to play for money.
    (a)   Who persuaded him?
    (b)   What was the priest going to do if he won any money?

14 Who was lucky at playing?

15 Why did the judge lose a lot of money on the last game before the train reached Tralee?

16 Who won the last game?

17 The judge went to the courthouse the next morning.
    (a)   What was his third case about?
    (b)   Who was the accused person in this case?
    (c)   Did this person say he was guilty or not guilty?

18 Lurgan Keane had been travelling on a train.
    (a)   Where was the train going?
    (b)   Why had Lurgan Keane called the police?
    (c)   What did the police find in O'Connor's pocket?

19 Who had spoken first on the train and why?

20 Who had suggested playing poker for matchsticks?

21 Who had suggested playing poker for money?

22 How much had Lurgan Keane lost?

23 Who had won the money?

24 Explain why the judge found O'Connor not guilty.

25 Lurgan Keane and Judge Comyn stood looking at an expensive car leaving the hotel.
    (a)   Who was driving the car?
    (b)   Who did the judge say was sitting in the car with O'Connor?
    (c)   Who did Lurgan Keane say was sitting in the car with O'Connor?

GLOSSARY

Glossary

1 **bored** (page 6)
   not interested in what is happening round about you.

2 **yacht** (page 6)
   Mark Sanderson is very rich and owns many of the things owned
   by rich people. One of these is a sailing boat which is called a
   yacht.

3 **simple** (page 6)
   plain – not rich and expensive.

4 **call for** (page 7)
   to call for someone is to come to that person's house to take them
   out.

5 **old-fashioned** (page 7)
   not modern and up-to-date.

6 **divorce** (page 9)
   when a husband and wife go to court and say that they no longer
   want to be married.

7 **fiercely** (page 9)
   Sanderson spoke with a lot of power in his voice.

8 **obsession** (page 9)
   a person who has an obsession keeps on thinking about the same
   thing all the time.

9 **rent** (page 10)
   to rent a house or a flat is to pay money to live there. The money
   is often paid before you start to live there. Sanderson paid two
   months' rent in advance.

10 **blond** – *dyed blond* (page 10)
   Sanderson changed the colour of his hair by dyeing it a fair
   colour.

11 **soldier** – **mercenary soldier** (page 10)
   a mercenary soldier fights for any country or army which pays him
   money.

12 **bastard** (page 11)
   a word used as a strong insult. (A bastard is someone whose
   parents are not married.)

13 **Earls Court** (page 11)
   a part of central London where there are lots of bars and cheap
   hotels.

14 *scar* (page 11)
a mark on a person's body left by an injury in a fight or in an accident.

15 *siesta* (page 14)
people who live in hot countries often have a short sleep in the afternoon. This sleep is called a siesta.

16 *stationer's* – *stationer's shop* (page 15)
a shop which sells different kinds of paper, pens and pencils, sticky tape, glue etc.

17 *reserved* (page 15)
you reserve a room in a hotel by asking the booking clerk to keep a room for you. A single room is a room for one person only. You confirm your booking by sending a letter. When you leave a hotel, you have to check out. You also confirm an airline booking. Most airlines ask you to reconfirm your booking for your return journey. (see Page 17).

18 *passport* – *false passport* (page 15)
you use a passport with your photograph in it when you are travelling from one country to another. A false passport is one which is not a real passport. Someone has made it to look like a real passport. Criminals often use false passports.

19 *dock* (page 19)
a ship docks when it comes into harbour. The cargo doors are opened and lorries drive off the ship through the cargo doors and onto the dockside.

20 *customs shed* (page 19)
when lorries arrive from a foreign country, the goods in them are checked by customs officers. The officer checks the driver's papers – import documents – and inspects the contents of the lorries to see how much tax must be paid. Also many goods are not allowed to be taken from one country to another – for example, illegal drugs and guns.

21 *mechanic* (page 19)
a mechanic is a person who knows how to repair engines. A mechanic will also bring extra parts – spare parts – for an engine in case they are needed.

22 *binoculars* – *a pair of binoculars* (page 20)
you hold binoculars in front of your eyes, so you can see things clearly in the distance. (They are like two small telescopes joined together.)

23 **hell** – *what the hell* (page 22)
    words which are used to show very strong surprise. The other
    driver cannot understand why Liam is still in the customs shed.

24 **Garda** (page 22)
    the police in the Republic of Ireland are called the Garda.

25 **overtake** – *overtook* (page 22)
    when one car goes faster and goes ahead of the car in front, it
    overtakes the other car.

26 **barn** (page 23)
    a large building used for storing hay or corn on a farm. It has wide
    doors and is big enough for a lorry to go inside.

27 **fertilizer** (page 24)
    farmers put fertilizer on fields to make their crops grow better.
    Natural fertilizer is made from manure – cow dung – which is why
    the policeman laughs.

28 **waste** (page 26)
    to waste someone's time is to make them pass time doing
    something without any profit.

29 **straw** (page 26)
    dry stalks of wheat used by farmers as beds for animals.

30 **shut up** (page 28)
    to stop talking suddenly and completely.

31 **bazooka** (page 28)
    a powerful weapon, like a large gun, made out of a round tube.

32 **hijack** (page 28)
    to steal a lorry load of goods while it is being driven from one
    place to another.

33 **clinic** – *an expensive clinic* (page 29)
    a small hospital which is often private and costs a lot of money. A
    doctor has an office in a clinic. The doctor in this clinic tells
    Timothy Hanson that he is very ill with cancer and is going to
    die in six months' time.

34 **will** – *make a will* (page 29)
    a paper which a person writes before they die. In this paper, the
    person says who is to get their money and their property when
    they die.

35 **nun** (page 29)
    women who live together, and spend their time praying to God
    and helping people who are poor or ill, are called nuns. In this
    story, the nuns help children who are orphans– children who
    have no mother or father. The Mother Superior is the woman in
    charge of the nuns and the orphanage.
36 **waggle** (page 29)
    children are rude to one another by putting the thumb of one
    hand to their nose and moving their fingers about– waggling their
    fingers.
37 **burial** (page 32)
    a burial takes place when a dead body is put under the ground in
    a graveyard. But a body can also be buried at sea. Timothy
    Hanson has asked to be buried at sea.
38 **estate** (page 32)
    everything which belongs to someone who has died is called their
    estate. In Britain, there is a tax put on everyone's estate.
39 **lead** (page 32)
    lead is a very heavy metal which is not very valuable.
40 **platinum** (page 36)
    platinum is a very heavy metal which is very valuable.
41 **furnace** (page 36)
    a stove in which metals can be made so hot that they melt – turn
    into a liquid.
42 **dealer** – *scrap metal dealer* (page 37)
    a person who makes money from buying and selling old, broken
    pieces of metal. If dealers buy and sell in cash and not in cheques,
    they can avoid paying tax and so make more profit.
43 **Guernsey** (page 37)
    an island between England and France. Someone leaving money
    in his will in Guernsey does not have to pay tax on his estate.
    (See Glossary no. 38 above.)
44 **compartment** – *first class railway compartment* (page 40)
    an expensive and comfortable part of a carriage on a railway
    train.
45 **patience** (page 40)
    a game of cards played by one person by her/himself. The cards
    have to be put down in a certain order. If the player has no cards
    left in her/his hands, they have won the game.

46 **poker** – *a hand of poker* (page 41)

poker is a game of cards usually played for money. Each person is given five cards by the dealer. These five cards are called a hand of poker. Each player is then allowed to change three cards. The players then bet money and the aim of the betting is to deceive the other players, so that each one does not know how good a hand the other players have. In the last game played on the train, the judge is sure he must have the best hand because he has four queens – an unusually good hand. But he is beaten by the priest who has four kings.

47 **luck** (page 42)

Gamblers often believe in luck. A person who has good luck wins at cards and a person who has bad luck loses.

48 **sin** (page 42)

a sin is something you do that is wrong. Some religions teach that it is a sin to play cards for money.

49 **charity** (page 44)

to give money to help poor people is to give money to charity.

50 **against** – *case against* (page 45)

O'Connor was arrested by the police because they found in his pocket a pack of cards used by people who cheat at cards. O'Connor was taken to court and accused of cheating. This is the case against O'Connor.

51 **proved** (page 47)

The judge has to decide if O'Connor is guilty or not. O'Connor shows that he did not cheat because he did not win any money. It was an unknown farmer who won all the money. So the case against O'Connor is not proved.